# Ice Skating

## A Level Two Reader

By Cynthia Klingel

The Child's World®

Ice skaters glide smoothly over the ice. It looks so easy to do!

Ice skating is a fun sport. You can skate on outdoor ice rinks in the winter. You can skate on indoor rinks all year long.

The main thing you need to ice skate is a pair of skates! An ice skate is a special boot with a sharp blade on the bottom.

Ice skates must fit well and support your ankles. Don't forget to lace your skates properly.

It is also a good idea to wear gloves or mittens. It is easy to fall when you are learning to skate. Mittens protect your hands when you fall. Mittens also keep your hands warm!

It is important to warm up your muscles before you skate. Do a few stretches with your arms, your legs, your neck, and your waist.

13

You are ready to skate!
Stand on the ice with your
heels together and your
toes pointed out in a V.

Start by taking small marching steps. This will take practice!

Your arms should be out at your sides. This helps you keep your balance.

Your marching steps become smoother and smoother. You are ice skating!

# Index

# To Find Out More

**Books**

Blackstone, Margaret, and John O'Brien. *This Is Figure Skating.* New York: Henry Holt & Company, 1998.

Eckart, Edana. *I Can Ice Skate.* Danbury, Conn.: Children's Press, 2002.

Feldman, Jane. *I Love Skating!* New York: Random House, 2002.

Morris, Ann, and Nancy Sheehan. *Little Skaters.* New York: Grosset & Dunlap, 1997.

**Web Sites**

**Visit our homepage for lots of links about ice skating:**
*http://www.childsworld.com/links.html*

*Note to Parents, Teachers, and Librarians:*
We routinely verify our Web links to make sure they're safe, active sites—so encourage your readers to check them out!

# Note to Parents and Educators

Welcome to Wonder Books®! These books provide text at three different levels for beginning readers to practice and strengthen their reading skills. Additionally, the use of nonfiction text provides readers the valuable opportunity to *read to learn*, not just to learn to read.

These leveled readers allow children to choose books at their level of reading confidence and performance. Nonfiction Level One books offer beginning readers simple language, word choice, and sentence structure as well as a word list. Nonfiction Level Two books feature slightly more difficult vocabulary, longer sentences, and longer total text. In the back of each Nonfiction Level Two book are an index and a list of books and Web sites for finding out more information. Nonfiction Level Three books continue to extend word choice and length of text. In the back of each Nonfiction Level Three book are a glossary, an index, and a list of books and Web sites for further research.

State and national standards in reading and language arts emphasize using nonfiction at all levels of reading development. Wonder Books® fill the historical void in nonfiction material for primary grade readers with the additional benefit of a leveled text.

# About the Author

Cynthia Klingel has worked as a high school English teacher and an elementary school teacher. She is currently the curriculum director for a Minnesota school district. Cynthia lives with her family in Mankato, Minnesota.

Readers should remember…
All sports carry a certain amount of risk. To reduce the risk of injury while ice skating, perform at your own level and use care and common sense. Never skate on a frozen pond or lake without an adult's permission! The publisher and author take no responsibility or liability for injuries resulting from ice skating.

**Published by The Child's World®**
P.O. Box 326
Chanhassen, MN 55317-0326
800-599-READ
www.childsworld.com

**Photo Credits**
© Barbara Stitzer/PhotoEdit: 10
© John Terence Turner/GettyImages/Taxi: 17
© Ken Redding/CORBIS: 6
© Michael S. Lewis/CORBIS: 5
© Mike Brinson/GettyImages: 21
© Nancy Sheehan/PhotoEdit: 13, 18
© Novastock/PhotoEdit: 2
© Randy M. Ury/CORBIS: 9
© Royalty-Free/CORBIS: cover
© Royalty-Free/Photodisc/GettyImages: 14

**Editorial Directions, Inc.:** Editorial Directions, Inc.: E. Russell Primm and Emily J. Dolbear, Editors; Alice K. Flanagan, Photo Researcher

**The Child's World®:** Mary Berendes, Publishing Director

**Library of Congress Cataloging-in-Publication Data**
Klingel, Cynthia Fitterer.
  Ice skating / by Cynthia Klingel.
    p. cm. — (Wonder books)
"A Level Two Reader."
Summary: Simple text introduces the fundamentals of ice skating and the equipment used.
  Includes bibliographical references and index.
  ISBN 1-56766-461-X (lib. bdg. : alk. paper)
  1. Skating—Juvenile literature. [1. Ice skating.] I. Title. II. Wonder books (Chanhassen, Minn.)
GV848.95.K55 2003
796.91—dc21                    2002015149